For all those who dream

It was a bright and sunny day in the village of Sunnysands. Chaos knew where he and his owner would be going. He could smell the surfboard before he could see it! Dogs had good noses for things like that! The surfboard wax that Rudy his owner used smelled so strongly of apples and cherries. Chaos loved it because it smelled nice and it meant that he was going to the beach!

"Goodbye Frog" Chaos said to the cat who sat by the front door.

"Goodbye Chaos" Frog replied "Have fun on the beach!"

They both watched Rudy load his surfboard onto his big 4X4, followed by Chaos who jumped into the back. The trucks big engine started as Chaos asked "What will you do today Frog?"

"Simple" meowed Frog "I'm off to have a nap!"

CHAOS WENT TO THE BEACH ON A SUNNY DAY.

FROG THE CAT WENT FOR A SLEEP.

At the beach you can have lots of fun. There were people playing bat and ball, making sand castles and flying kites. Chaos liked to chase the colourful kites as they swooped low. But he sometimes got in trouble because he would run over the sand castles!

Rudy told chaos to be good while he was surfing with his friend Ted the policeman. He watched them run into the bright blue sea with their colourful surfboards under their arms.

Chaos was glad that Ted was here because that meant his dog Hank would be here too. Hank was a proper Police dog who went to real Crime scenes and used his nose to help the Policemen and Policewomen.

Chaos soon spotted Hank running towards him with his tongue hanging out one side of his mouth. He looked like he had been having fun!

RUDY AND THE POLICEMAN RAN INTO THE SEA.

HANK CAME RUNNING TO CHAOS.

"Hello Chaos!" barked Hank "How are you?"

"Hello Hank" Chaos barked back "I am very well thank-you. What have you been up to?" Chaos thought Hank looked happy but tired too.

"Oh you know, chasing a red *Frisbee*™ that was being thrown around by the Bakers children. Lots of fun, but I need a rest now!"

Chaos had been right. Hank *was* tired.

They both sat and looked at the rolling waves as they came into the beach. They could see their owners on their surfboards gliding along the glass-like waves.

"Chaos" Hank said "Have you heard about the missing fishing nets?"

"No I haven't" said Chaos "Oh do tell more!"

"The fishermen down at the marina have had some of their nets stolen. My owner hasn't found any clues yet."

"Don't worry" barked Chaos "This sounds like a job for Chaos and Frog!"

HANK WAS TIRED FROM CHASING THE *FRISBEE*™.

HANK SAID THAT SOME FISHING NETS WERE MISSING.

When chaos got home from the beach he was tired. But he was also excited because he couldn't wait to tell Frog all about the new case they had to investigate! But Frog was still asleep! He was all curled up on the end of the bed. 'Lazy cat!' thought Chaos.

Chaos didn't want to wake him though, so he went to get his dinner instead. He was halfway through when Frog appeared, still yawning and stretching after his sleep.

"Did you have a good day?" asked Frog as he walked up to his food bowl.

"Yes!" Chaos said through a mouthful of food. Frog gave him a look that said 'Dogs manners are terrible!'

Chaos finished eating then told Frog all about the missing fishing nets.

"I think I should go take a look and see what I can find down at the marina" said frog.

"Good idea!" replied Chaos.

FROG WAS STILL ASLEEP.

CHAOS WENT AND HAD HIS DINNER.

Frog was like most cats. He liked to sleep all day and go out at night. Frog liked it at night because most places were quiet and there weren't many cars around. He spent most nights running around with his friends.

But not when it was raining. Like most cats, Frog didn't like the rain. Tonight was dry though and Frog could see all the stars and the big shining moon high in the night sky. Frog used the light from the moon to make his way to the marina.

All the pretty boats were on one side with their big white sails all rolled up so the boats wouldn't float away. On the other side sat all the smelly fishing boats. Frog jumped onto the first boat and had a look around but he didn't find anything. So Frog jumped onto the next boat but still didn't find anything. Then he heard someone say "Excuse me, but you might like to try the green boat at the end"

Frog looked up and saw that it was Simon the Seagull who was talking to him.

FROG JUMPED ONTO THE BOAT.

THE MOON AND STARS WERE BRIGHT IN THE SKY.

"Hello Simon" meowed Frog "Haven't seen you down here for a while"

"No, Frog" squawked Simon "I've been hanging around the fishing boats out at sea"

"So what is special about the green boat then?" asked Frog.

Simon the Seagull let out a little laugh as he flapped his wings "Well, it's the only boat that has people come down to it at night"

"I had better check it out then!" said Frog.

The green boat was the same as all the other fishing boats except this one didn't have any fishing nets! Frog climbed all over the boat. He sniffed around, jumped up high and squeezed through small holes looking for clues. Then, right at the back under a bench, Frog saw something that looked out of place. Frog pulled bits of paper out from under the bench using his claws. With Simon looking over his shoulder, Frog began to piece all of the bits together.

FROG CLIMBED ONTO THE GREEN BOAT.

WHAT IS UNDER THAT BENCH?

Can you help Frog put the pieces of the clue together?

Frog ran as fast as he could back towards home. He had some great news for Chaos! This was the clue that could lead to Chaos and Frog solving this mystery! Frog ran along fences and across walls. He ran under cars and over motorbikes. Frog finally weaved his way past the water sprinklers that were keeping the gardens green and sneaked past the Milkman.

When he burst through the cat-flap he found Chaos fast asleep in the middle of the Kitchen floor!

"Chaos" Frog whispered in his ear "I have a clue for you!"

Chaos awoke with a start. "Huh? Frog? Is that you?"

"I have a clue!" Frog repeated.

Chaos sat up and let out a big yawn. "Tell me!"

"I pieced together torn up bits of paper that I found on the boat with the missing nets" Frog said "It made up a ticket from the football match between Seaside FC and Blades United"

"Hmmmm" thought Chaos aloud "I know where those boys train"

"Where is that then?" asked Frog

"The beach!" barked chaos.

Frog ran along fences and walls.

Chaos knows where the players practice.

Later that day Chaos headed to the beach with Rudy after he had finished work at the Fire Station. The sun was starting to set, lighting up the sky orange and pink. Chaos sat patiently while Rudy got his wetsuit on.

"Let's turn your video camera on shall we" said Rudy as he reached down to switch on the little video camera that he had attached to Chaos' collar "Maybe you'll catch me on some waves this time!"

With the camera on, Rudy ruffled Chaos' head and ran off to the sea with his surf board under his arm.

Chaos had other plans though. He trotted off up over the sand dunes. He hoped he wasn't too late to catch the footballers! He slowly sneaked to the top of the dune and peered over... and saw the football team practicing on the sand.

'Perfect!' thought Chaos. Then he spotted the bright red truck that they used. A plan formed in Chaos' head. So he quickly and quietly made his way to the truck and jumped in the back. He hid under a sheet and stayed still and quiet. Soon the players came back to the truck and then it started to move!

Rudy turned the camera on.

Chaos jumped into the truck.

It was a bumpy ride but Chaos stayed as still as he could. It wasn't long before the truck stopped and the engine went quiet.

Chaos listened for the sound of the doors opening and closing. He could hear voices growing quieter as they moved away from the vehicle. Chaos guessed that it would be safe now and jumped out too. A quick look around and a sniff of the air told him that they were at the marina. 'BINGO!' thought Chaos. He slowly made his way round some boats, following the sound of the voices. Then he spotted the footballers. They were taking a fishing net from a yellow fishing boat! Chaos hoped that the camera round his neck was catching this! What great evidence it will make!

They started to climb off the boat, so Chaos quickly ran back to the truck and hid under the same sheet as before. Where would they go next? Chaos thought he knew!

It was a bumpy ride for Chaos!

The players took the net from the boat.

Chaos was right. When the truck stopped again it was at the football pitches. The players were using the fishing nets as football nets! Now it all made sense! Chaos had to make sure that he had it all on tape.

He stood and watched them hang the net over the goal frame and start playing football. That was enough for Chaos, so he turned and ran the short journey home. He knew that Rudy would be angry with him for disappearing- But just wait until he saw the video!

Chaos was right again. When he got home, Rudy and Frog were waiting for him!

"Where have you been you naughty dog?!" said Rudy. "I've been worried about you!"

"Meow" added Frog as if to agree with his owner.

"Woof!" replied Chaos.

"Well, maybe that camera around your neck can help..." added Rudy.

They put the nets over the goals.

Rudy was worried about Chaos.

Rudy loaded the cameras memory card into the computer and began to watch the film. Rudy watched it all in silence. Then, when it had finished he ruffled Chaos' head and picked up the phone.

"Hi Ted. Can you pop round? I have something you might like to see... Ok... See you shortly then."

Rudy hung up the phone and went into the kitchen and made two cups of coffee. Then the doorbell rang. It was Ted the policeman. Rudy and Ted sat down with their cups of coffee and watched the video.

"Well, well" said Ted. "It looks like Chaos solved the case of the missing fishing nets!"

"I don't even know how he knew about it!" said Rudy.

"He's a very clever dog" said Ted "How did you know it was them?" Ted asked Chaos.

"Woof "said Chaos as he nudged Frog towards the two humans.

The two men looked at each other and laughed.

"I guess it's your cat that's the brains of this duo then!" laughed Ted.

Frog and Chaos loved the attention they were getting!

The men watched the video together.

Chaos barked and pushed Frog.

Ted the Policeman sorted everything after that. He went and told the footballers off and made them return the nets to the fishermen. The fishermen were glad to have their nets back. But they felt sorry for the football players who said they only 'borrowed' them because they didn't have any nets for their goals.

The fishermen liked football and were so glad to have their nets back that they agreed to buy the football team some new goal nets if the team agreed to have the name of the fishermen's boat on the football kit!

Everyone agreed and everyone was happy.

Ted the policeman warned the football players that they shouldn't borrow or take things without asking again.

"Sometimes" said the Captain of the green fishing boat "if you ask first, you might get what you want!"

They all agreed with the Captain.

The policeman told the football players off.

The fishermen were happy to have their nets back.

UNTIL THE NEXT MYSTERY...

The Real Deal!

Frog

Best Friends

Chaos (real name...Hank!)

10350786R00019

Printed in Great Britain
by Amazon.co.uk, Ltd.,
Marston Gate.